DREAMWORKS

DRAGONS
RESCUE RIDERS

THE MYSTERY OF THE DRAGON EGGS

Adapted by Maggie Testa

Ready-to-Read

Simon Spotlight
New York London Toronto Sydney New Delhi

SIMON SPOTLIGHT

An imprint of Simon & Schuster Children's Publishing Division

1230 Avenue of the Americas, New York, New York 10020

This Simon Spotlight edition January 2021

DreamWorks Dragons © 2021 DreamWorks Animation LLC. All Rights Reserved.

All rights reserved, including the right of reproduction in whole or in part in any form.

SIMON SPOTLIGHT, READY-TO-READ, and colophon are registered trademarks of Simon & Schuster, Inc.

For information about special discounts for bulk purchases, please contact Simon & Schuster Special Sales at 1-866-506-1949 or business@simonandschuster.com.

Manufactured in the United States of America 1220 LAK

10 9 8 7 6 5 4 3 2 1

ISBN 978-1-5344-8014-8 (hc)

ISBN 978-1-5344-8013-1 (pbk)

ISBN 978-1-5344-8015-5 (eBook)

The Rescue Riders
were gathering supplies.

Burple found lots of rocks.
He also found three
lost dragon eggs.

"Let's bring these eggs
home to keep them safe,"
said Winger.

Leyla looked in her dragon diary. "There are no blue-and-red eggs," she said.

They would have to wait
until the eggs hatched
to find out what kind of
dragons were inside.

Just then Chief Duggard
stopped by.
He needed a ride.

Dak and Leyla would take him on Winger and Summer. Cutter, Burple, and Aggro would stay home and watch the eggs.

Cutter, Burple, and Aggro began to argue because each of them wanted to be in charge of watching the eggs.

But then, they heard
a loud bang!
Something was outside!
It was a Slinkwing dragon.
He wanted to talk.

"Those are our eggs,"
he said. "We lost them.
We want to take them
home."

Burple, Cutter, and Aggro
felt sad for the Slinkwings.
They gave them the eggs!

After the Slinkwings left,
Cutter had an idea.
He would draw Slinkwing eggs
in the dragon diary.

Then the Rescue Riders
would know what
the eggs looked like.

Cutter opened the diary.
There was already a
picture of Slinkwing eggs.

They are green—
not blue and red.

The Slinkwings had
tricked them!
The Slinkwings would eat
the eggs!

Cutter, Burple, and Aggro
found the Slinkwings.
Aggro distracted them
while Cutter surprised them.

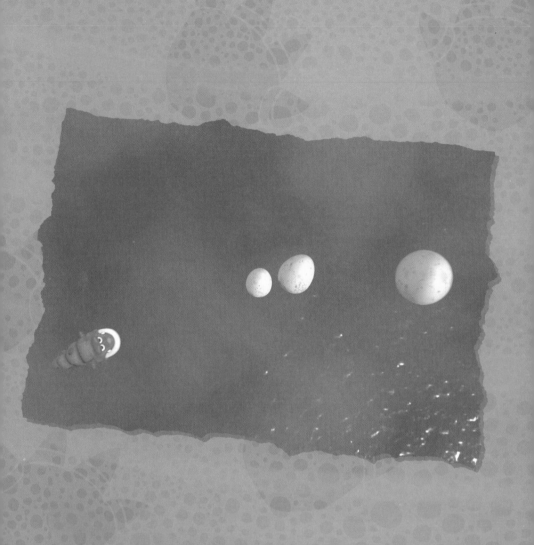

They dropped the eggs.
But Burple caught them!

He gave the eggs back.

But Burple had tricked them! He had replaced the eggs with rocks painted blue and red!

Burple brought the eggs home.

Before long,
the eggs started to hatch.
Baby Slobber Smelter
dragons came out.

They were home
with the best team
of Rescue Riders around!